To Avi, Naomi, and Noah with love

—DF

For my husband, Carlos Carrillo, for your love

—SS

 little bee books

An imprint of Bonnier Publishing USA

251 Park Avenue South, New York, NY 10010

Text copyright © 2017 by Douglas Florian

Illustrations copyright © 2017 by Sonia Sánchez

All rights reserved, including the right of reproduction in whole or in part in any form. LITTLE BEE BOOKS is a trademark of Bonnier Publishing USA, and associated colophon is a trademark of Bonnier Publishing USA.

Manufactured in China LEO 0617

First Edition   10 9 8 7 6 5 4 3 2 1

ISBN 978-1-4998-0462-1

Library of Congress Cataloging-in-Publication Data

Names: Florian, Douglas, author. | Sánchez, Sonia, 1983— illustrator.

Title: The Curious Cares of Bears / by Douglas Florian; illustrated by Sonia Sánchez.

Description: First edition. | New York, NY: Little Bee Books, [2017]

Summary: Illustrations and simple, rhyming text follow a family of bears from tree-climbing in spring, through all-night dances in summer, to their deep winter sleep. | Identifiers: LCCN 2016047312

Subjects: | CYAC: Stories in rhyme. | Bears—Fiction. | Seasons—Fiction.

Classification: LCC PZ8.3.F66 Cur 2017 | DDC [E]—dc23

LC record available at https://lccn.loc.gov/2016047312

littlebeebooks.com

bonnierpublishingusa.com

THE CURIOUS CARES OF BEARS

by Douglas Florian

illustrated by
Sonia Sánchez

 little bee books

The cares of bears
are curious indeed,

as you will discover,
if you care to read.

In springtime there's
carefully climbing up trees,

and stealing
the honey
from beehives
of bees.

There's chasing and racing
for hours and hours,

stopping from time to time just to smell flowers.

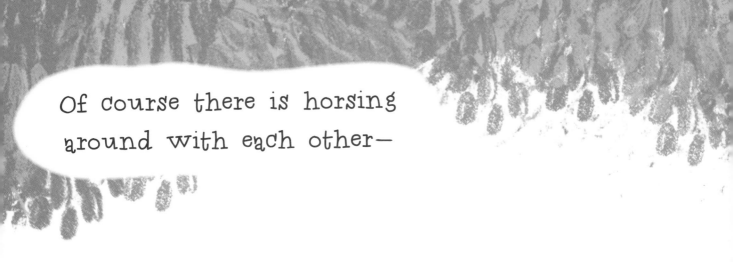

Of course there is horsing around with each other—

teasing your sister or wrestling your brother.

In summer there's swimming
inside of a creek,

playing jump rope or
perhaps hide-and-seek.

and feasting on berries, beetles, and bugs.

Then partying heartily, dancing all night;

howling and growling until morning light.

According to legend
bears care to go hiking

fifty-five miles or more,
then mountain biking.

then building a campfire
and sharing a song.

where deeply they sleep till
the springtime, and then . . .

and start to
explore the
wide world
with awe.